Unbinding

Mauro Paes Corrêa

UNBINDING

Mauro Paes Corrêa

Original Title in Portuguese: DESENLACE
First edition in English – 2022
Editing: Arial Books
Cover Design and Page Layout: Arial Books
Translation from Portuguese: Eduardo Aceves Campos | Arial Books

I.S.B.N. 978-65-00-39855-7
I.S.B.N. ePub 978-65-00-39856-4

Book and eBook available in

- Portuguese
- Spanish
- English

www.arialbooks.com

Proceeds from this work
will be donated to charity.

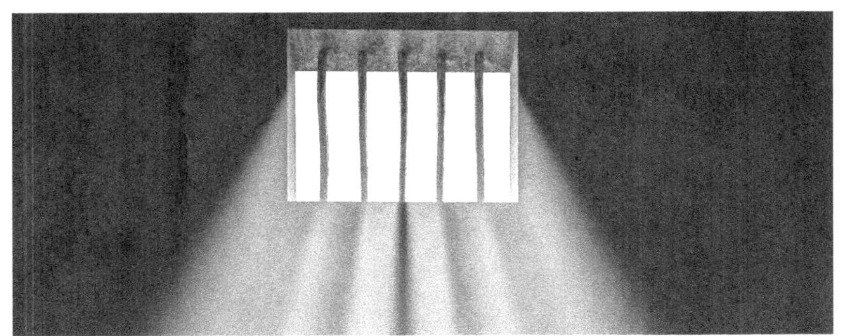

Unbinding

Mauro Paes Corrêa

It is not enough to stop doing evil,
it is necessary to do good
to free oneself and advance

Contents

Notes for the reader

Below is a brief explanation of some concepts that are mentioned in this book.

Spiritist Center

A Spiritist Center is a place to meet with friends who want to study the Spiritist Doctrine, pray, give and receive advice, give passes (placing hands on another person to transfer positive energies to those who are being helped), or who seek to make people positively change their way of acting and, if it is possible, that this can do good to the neighbor, all always through free will. This process is known as intimate reform.

Normally, once a week, the Spiritist Centers are open to the public who wish to seek information, study the doctrine, as well as request prayers, advice, food or any other kind of help. Anonymous charitable works are organized differently within a Spiritist Center, which welcomes all who seek them.

A Spiritist Center is not only a place to establish contact with spirits, but also, through mediums, that is, people who incorporate spirits either consciously or unconsciously, text messages (psychographed) or through voice (psychophonies) are transmitted.

Mediums don't evoke spirits. It is the latter who communicates spontaneously, because they know that in that place there are people with mediumistic sensitivity and are often authorized by Divine Grace to make some kind of manifestation.

With several case studies demonstrating the authenticity of messages to family members, as well as several other Spiritist works by different authors, it has been shown that Spiritism moves with science, and the idea of charlatanism disappeared many years ago.

Unbinding

The unbinding is the act of severing the link with the physical body, which occurs after death. Each person goes through a unique process of unbinding, because according to *The Spirits' Book* (Allan Kardec), the reception of the spirit in the spiritual life has many peculiarities.

The spirit is connected to the body through what is called the "silver thread or cord" (also called the fluidic thread, astral cord or fluidic cord), which is fixed from the moment of the conception of earthly life. The rupture of this "silver cord" determines the end of bodily life and occurs, in deaths from natural causes or diseases, a few hours after death. In sudden deaths, on the other hand, the cord breaks immediately after the end of bodily life.

The body does not suffer pain, but the spirit, especially if they are in areas of low vibration, such as the Umbral. As the spirit is often restored, its parts, limbs and their functions, such as walking, seeing and communicating, are also restored in some way.

The process of pain in the spirit is a learning process, just like pain in the physical body.

Colony of Flowers

Colony of Flowers is a spiritual colony that houses the spirits rescued from the Umbral, known as Purgatory or Hell in several religions. This colony is located in Brazil, above the state of Santa Catarina.

These colonies, in general terms, are slightly above the Umbral regions, as they can be a passing colony, if the spirit is evolved, or a colony of transition, to a new incarnation in the different worlds of the Universe.

As a rule, spirits, although unique, are linked to the same country or region at the time of the unbinding. Each country has different spiritual colonies.

All these topics are dealt with in *The Spirits' Book* and in greater depth in other Spiritist works.

Foreword

This spiritist novel was not psychographed. Inspiration came one night, in a manner unlike many others. The spirit friend, whom I might call "the Spaniard," suggested to me the plot of the book. "No era una mala persona, pero dejó de hacer el bien," he told me. He gave me enough inspiration to develop Alvaro's trajectory, the main character in this book. I dedicate this book to the noble spirit friend. May we, each in our own way, disseminate the Spiritist Doctrine.

This work is purely fictional. Any resemblance to reality is mere coincidence.

Umbral, 2007

He woke up to screams and shouts. Immediately, the headache persisted. For a brief moment, he thought he was still asleep, overwhelmed by the scene unfolding before his eyes. A stinking environment, small leafless trees, lakes of mud, and shapeless, hideous creatures. He was curled up in an almost fetal position when he woke up.

One of these creatures kicked him. It laughed mischievously. Much more frightening than the ones in horror movies, which he hated.

Alvaro had always been a logical man. If his head hurts, then he must be awake. In dreams, generally speaking, you do not feel the pain. This is what he read and heard from some acquaintances. What exactly was this place? The last thing he remembered was the hospital room, and the persistent headache that had been with him intensely over the last couple of months, because of brain cancer.

Even with his head pounding, and frightened by the Machiavellian creature's kick, he risks asking a question.

"What is this place?"

The shapeless creature stares at him, maliciously. It seems it is making an enormous effort to think about the answer.

"You are at the Umbral. You are people like us; you must have done all kinds of bad things on Earth. All those who do evil on earth come here or somewhere else. If you know what I mean."

"What is this all about? I died and ended up… here? What?" —alvaro is more frightened by his realization than by the creature's answer.

"Look, for your understanding... Your life on earth ended, now you are here. Do you understand? In the churches back on Earth, they say that this is Hell. Or, what is that name again? The Mansion of the Dead, that's it. I remember that from when I was a boy. And, you know what? You're very well-dressed. Were you a politician, a doctor? A lawyer? What did you do up there, huh? Did you steal from the poor? Forget it —he says, pointing to the other creatures—, they will tell us who you are. Better get used to it. I guess I welcomed you already, huh?"

It laughs aloud again, mocking the situation of Alvaro, who understood nothing. Alvaro decided to find a place far away to think. Even though everything smelled bad, in this discolored, tense and laden environment. He really was dressed up, in a suit and tie.

He walked for a few minutes until he found a large rock, which prevented him from being seen. His headache had increased.

How had he ended up there? He had never been a bad person. He was an ordinary citizen, an engineer, he had never meddled in other people's lives, and he had never done anything bad to anyone. What, he kept repeating to himself, had brought him to that place? It could not possible for him to be there. He never did anything wrong, he told himself. Of course, he was not perfect, but he always thought that if he died, life would end, or if for some reason there was an afterlife, he would go to a nice place.

While reflecting on the matter, another creature arrived. Wearing torn gowns, he seems to have the face of somebody with authority. It told him to stand up. He had a hard, serious, winning look, for this place anyway.

"So, my friend, I see you still don't remember me. I was almost certain, that you would throw your life away. We are of the same breed, but when I was incarnate, I knew exactly what I was doing. I gained power, manipulated people, and by the time I got here, I was not surprised by the place.

Alvaro was still scared. He did not remember that person at all. Answers nothing. His head hurts. It hurts a lot, he kept saying to himself.

The creature goes on speaking.

"In time, you will remember some things. Furthermore, you will remember others and me. Yeah, it will not be easy for you. Last time, you were rescued. It appears that someone interfered so that you did not stay here. So, you were reincarnated. As for me, I seem to be cut out for this place. Look, I have adapted so well, many of them I dominate and subjugate.

How did such a person know him so well? What did it mean with "throw my life away"? There were so many questions and only hideous or overpowering creatures, like that person, for the brief time he was there, that could answer them. Some of them looked as if they did not even have the ability to speak. He looked in the distance, shapeless creatures, and hideous faces, some without mouths, eyes, or ears. Others without body parts. Near him, creatures attacking others, hurting them in some way, continuously and mercilessly.

It was not possible, he lamented in the face of such a sad end. Where had he gone wrong? He never stole, never killed, never cheated, and always fulfilled his obligations. Where, he asked himself, where had he gone wrong?

Urussanga, 1943

The day was beginning to brighten in the Santana neighborhood in Urussanga, state of Santa Catarina, Brazil. Mr. Antonio and Mrs. Maria were waking up to the sound of trucks and miners passing by. Many of them descended from Italians who fled from the hunger and misery that devastated the northeastern region of what is now Italy. Other were Brazilians from several regions, who sought better life opportunities in the extraction of coal, the black gold, that had been moving the working-class neighborhood since the beginning of the decade.

Alvaro had been born in Santana, two years before that. He was the oldest son of the family, and would be joined by a sister born years later. Their little wooden house, despite being very similar to the others in the neighborhood, had been built in a small street, a little farther away. Mr. Antonio and his wife were not natives of the city; they had been born in Criciúma, a city in the southern region of Santa Catarina, which had been one of the most prominent since the 1900's.

They settled in Urussanga, motivated by the family patron's desire for a better life. Before that, he had worked in both farming and mining. Although it was hard work and quickly exhausted the lives of those who worked there, it was profitable enough to ensure the family's livelihood. An acquaintance who had heard that the city was in urgent need of labour for the new coal mines in various parts of the city interested him.

He gathered his only Cruzeiro, the currency of the time, and before the definitive move, he managed to buy a small house, sold to him by a man who had bought a bigger one, to better accommodate his growing family.

The move guaranteed Mr. Antonio a job. He was a thin man, but with the willpower and physical strength to endure the exhausting work. Thus, he gave Alvaro the opportunity of being born and living in the community until his teenage years.

During the years he lived in Santana, Alvaro behaved like an ordinary child raised in the 40s. The Second World War was raging abroad, and some people in the village were gradually persecuting the Italians. One could not speak Italian or any dialect, the gathering of men of Italian origin was not seen in a good way.

These situations did not affect Mr. Antonio's family. Firstly, because he was neither a direct nor an indirect descendant of Italians. Secondly, because he was a man who did not get involved in politics or other issues that did not concern him. He preferred to stay away from controversial issues or those that could bring problems to his family in the future.

In this environment, Alvaro had an uncomplicated childhood. Even though the lack of material goods predominated, once in a while, he had one meal a day. Her life was reasonably better than other people in the community, with larger families, where the sharing of bread, no matter how glorious, still reigned over malnutrition.

He had few friends, either in the neighborhood or in the village school, and was a boy of few words. An ordinary boy for his time. His physical beauty was not outstanding, since he inherited his father's genetic traits, as far as thinness, brown eyes, straight hair and nose.

You might say Alvaro was not shy either. He respected his father a lot, and he had given him good advice, such as studying and trying to avoid problems. It was better to be alone with his family than to have friends who could get him into trouble.

Mr. Antonio and Mrs. Maria had only one certainty when they considered the hard work of Antonio and the simple life they had led. Their son had to be able to advance in his education and later in society.

Alvaro was never a problem child. He never behaved poorly. He was not lazy, he always did the chores that his mother told him to do, such as sweeping the house, taking care of the chickens, the pig and weeding the small yard with a lime-orange tree and a small grape vine that Mr. Antonio planted months after Alvaro was born.

Going to school was a great milestone for Alvaro. He met new people, but he took with him the advice of his father to pay attention to school to achieve success in life. This gesture turned him into a quiet and obedient student.

In February 1950, Bruna was born. Alvaro's sister. Bruna was entirely different from her brother. Extroverted, talkative, challenged both parents from an early age. She did not behave as her parents wished, but since she was a little girl, she always showed her affection towards Alvaro. The seven years difference between the siblings made him an example for Bruna to be followed in some situations that life ended up reserving.

Perceptibly, this was the portrait common to millions of Brazilian families in those years. The only difference was the fact that Mr. Antonio and Mrs. Maria had only two children.

The neighbors, when there was an event in which the couple had to participate and bring their children, such as church or mining company events, always questioned the couple about the absence of more children. To the strangers, they would say that Maria could not have more children. In truth, the couple, even though they lived in simplicity and in harsh jobs, had managed to understand that it was much more worthwhile to raise their two children than to have a large family.

Even at the risk of one of their children dying from some contagious disease, so common in those days, such as measles, rubella, diphtheria, tetanus, whooping cough, infantile paralysis, infections due to wounds and bites from poisonous animals, such as snakes and spiders, common in that village.

Little by little, Mr. Antonio gained respect in the village. When Alvaro turned eighteen, in 1961, he decided to invest all his savings to pay for a college education for his son.

Alvaro was not a brilliant student, but he was hardworking. He always got average grades. Mr. Antonio, already retired from the mining company and suffering the consequences of working exhaustively for years in an unhealthy environment, made an appeal to his son:

"My son, today we have a good life. However, my health will not allow me to stay for a long time close to your mother and my daughter. My lungs are sick and, this shortness of breath that I have, the doctor said it would only get worse. So let us make a deal. You choose a major that will make you a doctor or some other prominent profession. My only wish is that you succeed in giving a better life to our family. In return, I will pay for all or most of your college education.

Alvaro, at the age of eighteen, was a responsible young man. He had not had a difficult adolescence; his personality had not suffered significant changes. At the same time, he was not popular with the girls, which allowed him to more readily accept his father's request.

He then decided to study Mechanical Engineering. He liked numbers and the calculations were logical, just like the gears. Other careers, such as lawyer, doctor, or any non-exact science, allowed different interpretations of a determined situation. He liked cold hard facts.

He had made his choice and informed his father. Satisfied with his son's choice, he told him to find out about the College Entrance Exam date for the course, which, in those days was only offered in the capital.

Mr. Antonio felt fulfilled. His son could have a life as comfortable as that of his superiors, many of them engineers. They indicated the locations of the black gold mines, the abundant coal in the region. When he left this life, whatever he found afterwards, there would be no feeling of remorse for having raised a failed son. Instead, in this village, he would be one of the few to lead their children to a better financial life.

Father and son understood each other perfectly regarding the matter. Bruna had just turned eleven. This was one of the factors in Antonio's decision to have a serious conversation with his son.

It would be natural for the father to have the firstborn guide his sister into her future. In his absence, he could control Bruna's strong temper without leaving aside his firm hand, in an attempt to guide his daughter to the right paths.

With the choice made, Alvaro studied hard for months to try to pass the College Entrance Exam in his first attempt. It was not an easy task, since most of the students had higher purchasing power, which made it easier to have access to tutors and private schools, without undervaluing the good teachers who passed through Alvaro's life. Public education at the time differed very little from private education.

Even the warm and suffocating afternoons of the summer in Urussanga did not discourage him. The city, receiving residents of other states, surprised visitors by the high temperature combined with the suffocating heat. Some said that the climate at this time was very similar to that of some cities in central Brazil, or even Manaus. A humid, almost viscous heat. As it arrived, it would leave in the first days of autumn.

He studied, as promised, and the exam was scheduled for January 1962, in Florianópolis.

Florianópolis, 1962

Alvaro was euphoric. After all, he was in the capital and if he was admitted, he would become a student in the first Engineering class of the newly formed Federal University of Santa Catarina (UFSC). He managed, through his father's acquaintances who had relatives or acquaintances in the capital, to find a place to live.

The place chosen was a student fraternity, which shocked Alvaro at first. It was a hodgepodge of voices, different people, and the most varied subjects that the voices disseminated among the walls of the building.

He was frustrated, at least in the expectation that he thought the place would be quiet enough to study. A young woman, who had arrived a few days before, approaches him in a friendly manner:

"Hey, you there! Are you lost?" she says, laughing, fraternizing with others with a glass of alcoholic beverage.

"I think so. I just got here. I've come to take the College Entrance Exam."

"What course?" she asks, curious.

"Mechanical Engineering. And what about you? Are you already enrolled?"

"No, no, I also came to take the exam. From your accent, you are Southern. Where are you from?"

"Urussanga, do you know it?" he says, as if talking about an unknown place.

She gives a loud shout, drawing the attention of the other students:

"Hey everyone, we have someone here from the land of Getulio Vargas' coal and wine! The gentleman here is from Urussanga!"

The students in the corridor laughed loudly and briefly at her outburst. The hubbub continues.

"Well, now I need to know where you're from. I think that's fair, don't you?" said Alvaro, somewhat disarmed by the girl's attitude and by the first sip of beer.

"I'm from Blumenau. My parents never got to keep me home. They thought it was better for me to go to school than to see me unhappy. I am like that, restless, playful, but I always wanted to study. For most men, I may be a different woman, but I do not think much of family nor children. I think about myself. I guess my thinking is selfish, isn't it?"

"I won't give an opinion. I do not even know your name!"

"Gabriela. And yours?"

"Alvaro, nice to meet you."

What both of them did not know was that the friendship between the two would be strengthened with the passing of time, mainly because that girl reminded him of his sister Bruna. Intelligent, uncontrollable and insatiable in certain aspects of life.

"Gabriela, how are we going to be able to study with all this commotion in this fraternity?"

"Calm down, my friend. May I call you that? It is just a welcome party, which will be repeated a couple of times. This is what college life is like. Nevertheless, there are more quiet days than with hustle and bustle and parties with booze and tobacco."

"Fair enough. I cannot disappoint my father."

"What do you mean you can't disappoint your father? Are you here only because he wants you to be?" she asks, annoyed.

"No. I am here for his wish and mine. Maybe at another time, I can tell you more about my story, and maybe you can tell me more about yours. Deal?"

"Deal! Urussanga guy." she says, laughing.

"My dorm, where is it?" he asks, still lost.

"You will see with the boys where there is a bed available. Here is practically communal and even if you do not like the attitude of some people, you will have to get used to it. Is that okay?"

"All right, no problem. I will see how I get around here."

Chatting with other boys, he discovered a bunk bed with an empty upper bunk. It was simple, like him. There would be no difficulty, as long as there was a study table or some other place to work as hard as possible. It was essential to pass on the first try.

He missed his parents. He should certainly find a job within a short time, which would pay at least for his trip to Urussanga. Moreover, Bruna, she was always on his mind. What would become of his sister without him?

He spent his first night in the fraternity struggling to sleep. The party lasted all night. Several colleagues were very drunk, and he assumed that some couples, brought together by drunkenness, had intimate moments, even too intimate.

When he woke up, he realized he was hungry. He had not eaten anything all day, since he had arrived at the bus station, straight to the fraternity house.

Other people were already awake or simply had not slept at all. He asked if there was any coffee.

“Here, you’re on your own. Everyone must contribute to the organization of the environment. There is a small fridge there and inside we have a weekly cleaning board. All food must be in containers with the person’s name on them. Those who have no name are discarded on housekeeping day. Right, newbie?” said one of them.

“Yes, I get it. So, that means that if I want to have my meals, I have to buy everything and then clean the place.”

“That’s about right, although some days the girls cook, and we help to clean the kitchen. The same can go for dinner. It is a way for us to keep the atmosphere sociable. We each buy something, and we put together a nice lunch or dinner.”

"Cool. Something positive, then. Thank you! By the way, what is the nearest grocery store or supermarket?"

"About ten minutes away. We are in downtown. You will find the establishments close by, right here on this street.

Alvaro went to the market. He bought bread, noodles, canned sardines and a small can of coffee. That would be sufficient to keep him going for the next few days.

To study, he elaborated a simple strategy: in the sorority, there was a shared study desk. He realized that most of the students were not as focused as he was on the seriousness of the exam. When available, he studied all topics in the examination. If there were no other option, he would study at a remote location on Mauro Ramos Avenue. The sorority was nearby.

He studied until the date of the exam, in the middle of April 1962. He took the exam very nervously as the last student to leave the room. He had unshakable confidence that he had gotten a significant number of questions right.

At the end of the month, the results were published. He was one of the approved students, half way down the list of engineering students. He was euphoric. He had to let his family know the good news.

From a public phone, he had called an acquaintance who lived in downtown Urussanga. He asked for someone to tell his parents that he had passed the test, and gave his parents his postal address.

"Alvaro, what a joy! I will certainly ask one of your father's acquaintances to take the message. Congratulations! So, we can have the opportunity to have a genuine Urussanga engineer?" said the gentleman on the other end of the line.

"Yes, as far as I am concerned, there is no lack of effort to face the challenge. Can you give them my postal address as well? You see, I am also writing a letter to them."

"Of course, young man. I wish you the best. Good luck with your studies!"

"Thank you, sir; I hope to visit my beloved city in the near future." He said, emotionally overwhelmed.

He ends the call and, at the same desk, tries to write a letter to his parents.

He calms his nerves and heart, takes a pen and starts writing the letter, to inform his family.

"My beloved parents,

I have passed the College Entrance Exam. My heart is radiant with joy. After all, I achieved my goal, which was to enter this disputed career. I am living in the sorority house, trying to think only about my studies. The future looks difficult, but when the difficulties appear on the way, I think a lot about dad, who struggled so hard for us.

I am worried about Mom and Bruna. I would like Bruna to answer this letter, telling me all the details about how everyone is going. I wish the best for all of us and that everyone is well.

I am sure you are already familiar with the good news, because I asked a friend of dad's to deliver the message. However, I thought it would be interesting to write to you all and inform you in more detail about the good news. I scored enough points to be approved. While I am on vacation, I plan to stay at Urussanga.

Regards,

Alvaro"

May 1962

It is the first day of school. He is nervous, restless. The halls of the newly opened Federal University are buzzing with conversations. New students, known as freshmen, exchange their first impressions. Alvaro is alone, leaning against a wall near his classroom.

There are still 20 minutes before classes start, enough time for Gabriela to find him.

"Hey Alvaro, are you happy?" she asks sincerely.

"Of course! If happiness means being nervous, I am happy. And you, how are you?"

"I'm fine. I think I am, in a way, fulfilled. We are starting the beginning of our days here, don't you think?" She smiles and winks at her friend.

"Of course, of course. It will be a long four years of studies. We will have to put up with each other." he replies, in an attempt to keep his good humor and nervousness at bay.

"So, Alvaro, we are going to have a little party at the sorority, what do you think about going?"

"I don't know, I think it would affect my academic performance..."

"No way, you silly. We will have beers, we will tell jokes, and we will have a little fun. Just a little distraction!"

"You are right; some fun is a way to celebrate that precious victory."

"All right. I am going to meet my friends. It was good to see you!" she says goodbye, kissing Alvaro on one cheek.

She leaves and blushes a little. He is not used to such intimacy with women. He is a little surprised. He had not thought that he had given her such freedom. Anyway, it was still a nice surprise.

He attends the first class, with the participation of the Dean, who welcomes the students and talks about the importance of the students for the economic, social and financial life of the State of Santa Catarina and the cities where they will work, should they manage to finish their courses.

After the Dean's lecture was over, one of the professors explained how the student evaluation method works, the timetables, the University rules, and the sanctions in case of non-compliance with any rule.

Alvaro listened carefully to all the words that everyone spoke. It was an important day for him, and he insisted on sitting at the first desk so he could follow and absorb as much knowledge as possible.

By the end of the class, he had completely forgotten about Gabriela's invitation. When he got to the sorority, he heard the noise of the schoolmates at the entrance.

The party, he remembered. He looks for Gabriela, the one person with whom he is most intimate. He finds her, along with other colleagues of hers. They are all having a beer and a soda.

"Alvaro! How did your first class go?"

"I liked it so much that I promised myself that I would always sit in the first desk" says, laughing with happiness.

"Great. Do you want to sit with us? Enjoy, because you are the only man around with four other women."

"I'm feeling important. Come on, Gabriela. It is a pleasure to be here. Thank you for the invitation."

They talked throughout the night, on the most varied topics, while drinking beer. When the beer was over, someone brought whiskey. Alvaro became intoxicated. It was a different sensation, of loss of self-control. Anaesthetic, with a feeling of freedom in the art of speech and thought.

He became uninhibited. The women seemed to pay attention to him. He had never noticed this detail before. It becomes more daring over the hours. They laugh, and so does he, about anything they say. The ethyl hypnosis takes them all away from rationality and sense of limits.

At the end of the night, Alvaro calls Gabriela. She responds, goes with him to the back of the house, going out through a small door, which gives access to the small back yard.

He kisses her very deeply. She accepts a scorching kiss. The unmetabolized alcohol is still acting in their bodies. He dares a little more. He presses his body against hers. He hears something like a moan.

Instinctively, he goes to the small house where the housekeeping and repair supplies are kept. They have wild sex, totally intoxicated. He had lost his virginity, with his friend.

They return to the sorority house as if nothing had happened. The lucid spectators (there were some) noticed the smeared lipstick on their mouths, the disheveled clothes, and the certainty that they were somehow involved. In the sorority, there is an underlying rule: that each one is responsible for his or her life, which led to the incident having practically no repercussions because at parties, there was always some event similar to what happened to the two of them.

Alvaro falls into bed exhausted, in every respect. He sleeps until seven o'clock in the morning the next day, waking up with a terrible, throbbing headache. He had never felt this way before. Not only did his head hurt, but his stomach did too.

He took an aspirin from his belongings and went to make his coffee. Since he had never been drunk before, he asked one of his colleagues, who was sharing the table, about the pain.

“So, Alvaro. Every action has a reaction. What you are going through is called a hangover.”

“Is that right? So, you mean that every time we drink in excess, the organism reacts in this way?”

"Exactly. Moreover, the ingestion of alcohol is harmful to the organism."

"Why do you say this?"

"You see, I come from a Protestant family. We know how bad alcohol is for people. I am a teetotaler. Do you know what this is?"

"No, can you tell me more about it?"

"It means that I don't drink. I do not harm my body; we think that alcohol is harmful to the body. The one who gave us the body is God, and the act of harming it is an affront against the Father."

"You have a religion full of rules, so..." he says, still waiting for the effects of the aspirin.

"Yes, discipline is important for the human being. So is faith. By the way, do you have a religion?"

"Me? I think I am Catholic. Honestly, I have never really believed in these things. Miracles, life after death, deliverance, things like that. I am very rational."

"So you are an atheist?"

"Maybe I am. I believe in family values, that's for sure."

"Don't you think that we are eternal?" the colleague asks, defiantly.

"I don't think anything. I live reality, the here and now. If I have frustrated you, I apologize. Thanks for the lesson on alcohol."

He leaves the table and goes back to bed. He still does not feel well. Suddenly, he remembers that he had a thing with Gabriela, but does not know exactly what it was. What is more, he is ashamed to ask her. Anyway, when he gets better, before going to class, he will ask her.

Anyway, he made the decision that when he drinks, he's not going to overdo it. Not at all. He didn't find it at all interesting to lose his sense of self, no matter how pleasurable the feeling was initially. It is important to remain lucid, he told himself.

The aspirin takes effect; he gets up, now with more energy. He decides to look for Gabriela. He walks around the house and does not find her. She is probably already awake and busy with other things.

He has a feeling of concern about Gabriela, but does not yet know exactly why.

During the day, he finds her. She calls him, with her forefinger, far away from everyone.

"Hey Alvaro. You know what happened yesterday, right?"

"I don't know, Gabriela, I guess." We crossed the line, didn't we?"

"Oh, yes, we did. We made love there in the little house. Did you like it?"

He is completely speechless. He apologizes to the girl, saying that it was not his objective to take her virginity or to be rude to her. He was drunk. He makes a big apology.

"Don't worry, I'm not a virgin and it was just a fun night out. I just hope I do not get pregnant because I realize you have never had a woman. Are we still friends?"

"Yes, yes. If you want, of course."

"You silly boy, of course I want to. What happened yesterday was an organic necessity. I think you understand, don't you?" she laughs at his innocence.

Alvaro continues his days, studying hard and with a lot of willpower, getting good grades and at the end of the semester, advancing in all subjects.

Santana, New Year's Eve 1962 - 63

He went back to Urussanga during the December break. He found his old father sicker and his mother still devoted to family chores.

They spend Christmas and the last week of the year in peace. He talks a lot with Bruna, who for days asked him to tell her everything that happened during the months he stayed in the capital. He tells her everything she needs to know.

She is excited, her brother somehow manages to control that vivacity of hers in the form of rebellion. This is what she has always dreamed of, getting out of there and having an independent life, when she arrives at the age of her older brother.

"Brother, do you believe that I can go further, like you?"

"Of course, Bruna. Have I ever told you anything different? If it wasn't for Dad, I couldn't have gotten this far. When I graduate, I believe I can be employed and be able to do the same as Dad is doing for me. This is the meaning of family. And also to provide us with greater comfort. How is Dad?"

"Not good. I spoke with his doctor. He said he would not last long. His lungs are much compromised. This disease from the mine is fatal."

"I'm worried about him too, but I avoid asking any questions. I notice he is trying to act as if he is fine or he is trying to control himself as much as he can if he is in pain. Is it not possible that we can look for another doctor to help him?"

"You see, Alvaro, I asked the doctor the same question. He himself told me that he had consulted other colleagues, showed them Dad's radiological exams, and they all came to the same conclusion. He'll hardly pass 63."

Alvaro is sad, and he notices the same in his sister's speech. As a way to compensate for his absence, he tries to have all meals with the family.

On New Year's Eve 1963, they all spend time together in the house in Santana. The neighborhood, the people, is all the same, as if it was an immobile picture of a reality that would not change for a long time. His father bought a sparkling wine and at midnight they popped the cork. They were celebrating their firstborn son's success in his studies.

The next morning, the father asked to talk to his son privately.

He goes to meet his father. Maybe he has some advice for us or some reflection.

"My son, I am very happy for you. My reason for our conversation is about my health. Unfortunately, it has worsened. I secretly went to the doctor and asked about my situation. He tried to deny it, but I told him that the engineers down at the mine say that doctors must tell the truth, according to the oath taken by a man named Hippocrates. I think that's the name. That made him embarrassed. He told me the whole truth. I must have at most one year to live. Since I am still lucid, I talked to an engineer I worked with before I got sick. He told me that I should make a will and leave everything divided up. I talked to your mother and she agreed. You know I cannot just walk out of here and leave you with nothing. Since you will continue studying and the money that I have set aside will allow you to complete this stage, I will leave it in writing that you have a right to the house. The engineer said that it is law, as well as right into the savings. However, you must agree that they will use the house as long as they are alive or single. Your mother and Bruna will get married one day."

"Don't say that, Dad, don't even think about it! You are there alive and already thinking the worst. All right, I agree with everything. Do as you see fit. I think a lot about you and them in the capital."

"I know this, my son. My faith in God allows me not to be selfish. You believe in God, don't you, son?"

"Father, I was asked the same question one day in the capital. I said that I am very rational. I believe in facts and science."

"It's a shame my son, believing in God makes us bear the challenges of the journey. I hope that one day you will believe in Him. So, are we done?"

"We are. You are a great man. Thank you for dedicating your life to us."

"I've done nothing but my duty. Now go there, take care of them."

He leaves, sad. He was not aware that his father already knew the real picture of his situation. Now the need to support the family is even greater. He was not prepared for that, but he would handle the situation to the best of his ability.

Thereza, March 18, 1963

He was in the capital again. His father died unexpectedly. It was up to Alvaro to organize all the funeral arrangements, and sadness still invaded him constantly. In the second semester, he continued to study in the same way, but cutting back on excessive drinking. He created a method called "face scratching". He heard from a friend that when you scratch your face and do not feel the contact, you are drunk. Before he lost this sense, stops the consumption of alcohol. At every party, he has proceeded this way and has had no further contact with Gabriela. Not in the intimate way, obviously.

On March 18, Monday, the school year started. There were new students in the other semester, and the freshman class made their introductions.

Alvaro's attention was immediately drawn to that tall, thin, brown-eyed woman with flame-colored hair. It seems to have an authentic vibrancy.

With the excuse that he is just introducing himself, he tries to lengthen the conversation with Thereza. She introduces herself, says she is from the capital itself, from a middle-class family, and loves Engineering. Presumably, she found the conversation interesting, as she told some details about her private life, with special attention to her volunteer work.

"Alvaro, isn't it? Sorry, your name doesn't seem to fit you. Anyway, my parents have always encouraged me to study. In my spare time, I try to practice charity and take part in a Spiritist Center, helping in its work."

"Spiritist Center, what is that? It reminds me of African religions…"

"No, nothing like that. We have deep respect for religions, all of them. A Spiritist Center is a place for studying the Spiritist Doctrine and encouraging the practice of charity, as well as the teachings of the master Jesus."

"Funny, never heard of it" he says, really curious.

"Alvaro, do you believe in God?"

He recalls other conversations where they were asking for exactly the same thing. It is almost a coincidence.

"No, I don't believe, I'm too rational, that's why I chose to study engineering."

"Well, I hope that one day our course will make you wonder if behind all the gears, God is acting behind the scenes. I have a lot of faith, not only in God, but in Jesus, and I value all and any act that seeks to bring good to people, not only materially, but spiritually."

"Congratulations. That is beautiful."

"Don't you want to go there with me one day?" she asks.

"Thereza, I'm sorry, but I don't think that's my area. I cannot lie to myself if I do not have faith. I cannot fool myself. That is what I can express to you now."

"All right, Alvaro, anyway, it's a pleasure to meet you. We will see each other a lot more," she says with absolute certainty about the future.

He has a good impression of the girl. It is a pity that he does not share her opinions. Still, she is a good woman; he repeats this to himself several times.

Alvaro does not know that Thereza is a woman with a haughty spirit, detached from materialism, self-sacrificing in doing the most for everybody else, even though she comes from a family of mostly materialists.

Some friends introduced Thereza to the Spiritist doctrine. She found no explanation in other religions or in books about the perceptive gift she immediately sensed in some people. Some she perceived more overtly, others a little less. And some totally fooled her.

When she attended her first lecture on the Spiritist doctrine, she got to know The Spirits' Book. There she found the answer to so many questions she had asked herself during her adolescence! So, that was it! Life is evolution, the spirit is eternal and death is just a stage, a practical school of spiritual evolution.

She told her parents about her adherence to spiritism and was surprised to find no resistance.

"Dear daughter, if that is where you find the strengthening of your faith in God, keep going. It does not disqualify us at any moment and in any way, you opting for a religion different from ours. The important thing is for you to be a good person."

"Dear Dad, thank you for your understanding. I want to continue to work for the underprivileged and as secretly as possible, I find it inconsistent to do good and talk about these acts all over."

"Truth, daughter. In the Bible, we can see that those who did this were the Pharisees. Jesus said that the good we do to our neighbor is a way of loving him. Follow what your heart is saying."

They hugged each other emotionally. From that day on, with the support of her family, she dedicated herself constantly to the study of spirituality and the practice of good.

She immediately liked Alvaro. She does not know the reason or his origin, but he is a good man. No one could condemn him for not believing in God, but he seems to have enormous affection for his family, which is a big step. She had high hopes that Alvaro, by his free will, would naturally perceive the existence of God and his mysteries on the earthly plane.

During that semester, she continued to meet with Alvaro almost daily, without talking directly about spirituality.

Alvaro felt he had a crush on the girl. A sweet, kind woman, with a sparkle in her eyes that he did not know.

There was a unique interest in him to ask her out, go to the movies, and listen to her voice talking about any subject.

At the end of the semester, he took the initiative to ask her out:

"Thereza, would you accept an invitation from me to go to the movies?"

"Of course, you are a gentleman. It will be a pleasure to have your company."

They go to the cinema, one of the most renowned in the capital. There is a symmetric energy between the two, even if they do not realize it. For Thereza, there is a vital mission there, which the veil of oblivion prevents her from remembering. The same happens with Alvaro.

As they leave the cinema, he looks with such love into those eyes that he kisses her tenderly.

"Thereza, I don't know what love is between a man and a woman, but if it's the desire to be together and enjoy every moment of your company, then I believe I love you. Would you be my girlfriend?"

"Alvaro, I have loved you for a long time. I can speak more precisely to this feeling because it lives within my heart. Yes, I accept."

"Even though I differ from you in many opinions and attitudes?" he asks, bringing his rational side to light.

"Alvaro, all of us here, first of all, are not perfect. We are here to learn from each other, and overcoming what you call defects is a natural stage of human life. Of course, I accept!"

They hug, kiss again, and walk hand in hand. Alvaro does not know it, but that is the first key moment that could free him from the Umbral, many years later.

The union of the two is only the beginning of a new development in Alvaro's life. For Thereza, it is the certainty of finding a sincere companion on her journey. In this aspect, Alvaro did not fail.

December 1966

It was Alvaro's graduation. She was in her last semester. They both met their families, making a good impression on everyone.

Bruna liked Thereza. So sweet, clarified on the facts of life, encouraging. Meanwhile, Mrs. Maria had disincarnated in 1965 from a sudden heart attack.

Her daughter was completely puzzled, as was Alvaro, who was worried about Bruna's situation. Whom would she stay with? Would she be able to stay alone in Urussanga?

At the end of May 1965, when Mrs. Maria had disincarnated, Alvaro consulted Thereza.

"My dear, Bruna is already seventeen years old. You see, you have your father's retirement money and savings; you can give your share to her. She is known in the community and the people are respectful. She will probably find a good man and continue her studies. Moreover, we will always keep in touch with her because I will only study for six more months and then we can move to Urussanga. You can work in the mining companies, there are jobs guaranteed for you."

"You are right, dear. But, do you think she will find a good man?"

"Very soon, be sure of that" she said, with that confidence he had given up on understanding.

During all the years they had been dating, he had never interfered in the work she was doing at the Spiritist Center and had asked nothing about it.

She did not touch the subject directly either, believing in the power of free will.

She realized that Alvaro had every opportunity to do good, but did not do it. It was not the fact of doing evil that worried her, but the absence of his impulse to do good. She prayed every night that her boyfriend would seek the path of elevation.

The graduation, as it could only be, was very emotional for him. He remembered his parents, the unimaginable effort of the patriarch to endure the exhausting work in the mine, thinking only of the family. If he had a son, he would name him after his father. It was an irrevocable decision that no one could take away from him.

Bruna was also at the event. Everybody stayed at Thereza's parents' home, who were very happy to meet their daughter's boyfriend's only sister. She was enchanted by the family and the city. She had never been to Florianópolis and, at some point in her life, she had to follow in the footsteps of her older brother.

After graduation, there was a dinner at Thereza's family home. Her father was very happy for his daughter's boyfriend.

Alvaro felt fulfilled. He felt blessed to have a wonderful girlfriend, good parents, and his sister absorbing the kindness of Thereza and her parents.

During the week of graduation, he had bought an engagement ring. As soon as he got a job, with a fair salary, he would marry Thereza. He felt ready to get married to Thereza.

At dinner, while the toast was being made with juice, he asked everyone for permission to speak. Taking advantage of his graduation clothing, he stands up and says, without planning anything, the following words.

"My future father-in-law and mother-in-law. I truly love your daughter and am interested in marrying her. I would like to ask for your daughter's hand in marriage. Do you accept?"

The in-laws cry with happiness, Thereza cries in a mixture of surprise and joy. Bruna, although she had her tough way, hidden in that beauty as striking as Thereza's, also cries with joy.

The patriarch, acts like a very happy host:

"Of course, Alvaro. I agree, and I believe my wife also agrees, with your request. However, I want to remind you that the decision is Thereza's alone."

Thereza says nothing, hugs Alvaro and exposes her hand for him to slowly place that beautiful ring on his finger. She touches it, knowing that it will accompany her for life.

"My dear, there are moments when nothing needs to be said, the action speaks for itself. Thank you, I have been waiting for this moment for a long time. I really want to form a family with you and it is a joy to have Bruna as part of it."

Still, at the end of the year, he returns to Urussanga, sounding out some companies about the possibility of a job for him. He returns not only with one offer, but with three. With Thereza, he picks the most interesting one, as they both have the same taste for engineering. He chose one of them and decided to move in January of the following year, while Thereza was studying for another six months in the capital.

During that period, he will live in Santana, with his sister. It is an opportunity to work and at the same time organize his future life, while taking care of her sister, who, despite being sweeter as the years go by, still shows a wild or rebellious temperament in certain situations.

Urussanga, 1967 - 1970

Finally, Thereza had graduated. The years go by, transforming her into a woman more and more devoted to charity. Alvaro, on the other hand, looks like a dead rock. The fraternal work of his wife does not seem to move him, even though he considers the gesture of the bride very noble.

They decided to marry in Urussanga, a month after he graduated. She was very happy, radiant. Alvaro and Bruna made all the arrangements.

Socially, Thereza had more friends than Alvaro, not only because of her social circle, but also because of her volunteer work. Neither of the guests refused to go into town to celebrate the couple's wedding.

The wedding was a rare occasion where there was some kind of friction between the parties. Thereza wanted the wedding celebrated in a religious and doctrinal fashion. Alvaro thought a celebration of civil marriage would suffice.

With a lot of patience and arguments, Alvaro accepted that one of the coordinators of the Spiritist Center of Florianópolis would perform the blessings and a short talk about the importance of marriage in spirituality.

Once convinced, Alvaro placed Thereza's wish on the festive agenda. In the meantime, Alvaro found a house downtown for them to live in. Bruna would go along and Santana's house could be rented to a miner, as a way to increase the savings for the youngest of the family.

The party took place on a Saturday morning in September. The weather was beautiful and the time was chosen so that everyone could return to the capital the same day. Ninety people were invited, most of them Thereza's friends. She was dressed in a white suit and he was wearing an elegant gray suit. Both were dressed appropriately for the wedding, without losing the simplicity of the act.

"Happiness in this world is not in material things," she said as she and Bruna were drawing up the guest list. Bruna asked her future sister-in-law the reason.

"In the Spiritist Doctrine, the understanding is that we must use material goods to primarily aid moral and spiritual evolution. Material things are one of the causes of the disorder and even of the attachment of spirits to the earthly plane."

"Do you mean then that the spirits can really continue here on earth?" she asks, wanting to know more and more about the subject.

"But of course Bruna! Let me give you an example: There are many spirits of people who have struggled all their lives to achieve material comfort. And then, they disincarnated. The problem is that instead of them working, or seeing work as a means of moral and intellectual elevation, they divert it to the accumulation of goods. Those who can't let go of them, are left watching fights at the moment of inheritance, over their goods, or even being impacted by the action of time, which is inexorable."

"How horrible! But, my father worked hard so that our family could have greater comfort. I was worried!"

"You see, your father's case is a little different. He tried to work and sacrificed his health, in a way, for his family. Was he ever greedy or overly concerned about his possessions?"

"No, Thereza. He just wanted us and Mom, to be ok. He was a man of great faith. Too bad you never met him. Speaking of which, Alvaro, what do you think about this?"

"Your brother has some resistance about it. However, I hope that life can open his eyes. I cannot interfere with his free will."

"Free will?" she asks, disconcerted.

"Yes, Bruna. God gave us a fundamental ability. Non-interference in our actions. For every action, there is a reaction. Based on this logic, we can say that a wrongdoer must pay for his faults, just as a benefactor can benefit from his actions. Everything depends on the actions that we choose to do."

"Do you mean that believing in God is one of them? My brother seems to be an atheist..."

"Well, believing in God is a great start. Believing in the eternity of life and in the responsibility of our actions is also another important step. However, there are people who, for some reason, do not believe in God and do charity in a selfless way. Sounds complex, doesn't it?"

"It is true. Nevertheless, are these people who don't believe in God and do good, in the same line of action and reaction?"

"Yes, dear, cause and effect. All of us who are on planet earth are brothers. Me, you, your brother, our parents, everyone, without exception."

"Wow! I didn't know that!"

"One day, there will be a Spiritist Center in this town. While it does not yet exist, when we go to the capital, I will invite you to attend a conference. The two of us can do the gospel at home, if you want, while you live with us. What do you think?"

"I think it's great, you do me a lot of good. I cannot explain it…"

"I love you like a sister too, dear Bruna."

Bruna loved what she had learned. She was definitely more mature.

The other day, as he was talking to Thereza and organizing the wedding details, Alvaro said:

"With you, Bruna seems more relaxed. What do you two talk so much about?"

"Women's business, my darling. Your sister is wonderful."

In June 1968, Antonio Neto was born. The couple's son was born physically perfect, but with some spiritual characteristics that will need Thereza's full support.

As a mother, she dedicates all the love necessary for the child and Alvaro is amazed at the genuine gift of being a mother that Thereza has.

Alvaro, just like his father, works incessantly. He accumulates material goods, thinks exhaustively about them, and about the most varied ways of expanding his estate. He devotes little time to his family, and on weekends, he leaves Thereza free to visit her parents or them to visit her.

They are new mines, new equipment, and other outside companies that observe his notorious commitment to work, and even research new techniques of coal exploitation, minimizing costs bringing more and more profits to the shareholders.

During the 1969 vacation in January, they spent the month with the parents of Thereza. In their typical volunteer work, at a conference, a medium receives an entity.

"Thereza, Thereza! How valuable has your work been all these years in this house. The spiritual benefactors have allowed me to bring you two messages. The first one is that you will have another son, very similar to his father. The firstborn will need constant care as to his spirituality. You have accepted to receive him as a son, in the form of a mission. The second son is the law of affinity in action. Similar to the father. However, with your dedication, you will achieve your intent to make him overcome the bad tendencies. As for your husband, try to bring him to the reality that the accumulation of riches does not bring benefits in the spiritual world. And when a Spiritist Center appears nearby, take him. For some reason, he will be convinced to go, but the result of accepting God and His laws depends solely on his free will. Go in peace, and may the benefactors accompany you."

Thereza was amazed. She had never received any messages, although she had witnessed countless mediumistic events, her focus was on working for others. She had always studied the Spirits' Book, the Gospel, and sought daily to improve herself. She did not expect a message from the spiritual plane, mainly about the future of his family.

On their way home, tactfully, she decided to talk to Alvaro, who was talking to his in-laws.

"Dear, can we talk a little later?"

"Of course. I'm free later, is everything okay?"

"Great, darling, thank you!" she kisses him on the forehead.

It was already nighttime and she was in bed, when he entered the room and closed the door.

"What did you want a little earlier, Thereza?"

"You know, I'm not a woman who asks for many favors. Would you do one for me?"

"Sure, dear, whatever you want. Do we need anything at home or for our son?"

"No, Alvaro. Can you go with me one day to the Spiritist Center?"

"Thereza, I admire your work, but you know my opinion on the matter. Why such insistence? I am a rational man, you know that."

"It's important to me. Could you at least go once?

Alvaro seemed not to like to touch the subject much, a fact that Thereza had noticed years ago. She, presently, seems to be determined. Her gaze seemed to need an answer, and he quickly realized the woman's reaction.

"Okay. This time I will go with you. Out of love and respect for you. This is the first and last time. Do we agree?"

"Yes, dear, just this once."

On Wednesday of the following week, taking advantage of her vacation, Thereza invites Alvaro. He accepts. They sit in one of the first rows, and Thereza listens patiently to the lecture. Alvaro even seems to show some attention, holding his wife's hand. At the end of the lecture, the lecturer, one of the founders of the center and also a medium, begins the mediumistic work. He incorporates in the medium, unconscious, the spirit of a woman, in her last incarnation.

"Beloved sister. Today you brought your husband. I thank you for your effort, and there is a message for him: change, man, your attachment to material goods, observe even in your work, the silent presence of God. The divine mercy, which acts in a unique way, has given you the chance to evolve morally. You are evolving intellectually, but I want to warn you that if your companion continues in the incessant search for materialism and notoriety as his sole objectives in life, he will have made a very serious mistake. This, his passage in earthly life, with your company, is to overcome this search, which has long ceased to be healthy."

Alvaro is extremely upset. Damn it! It is not possible to believe all this nonsense. He is a good, hardworking, law-abiding father. Everything he acquires is fair, so what is wrong with that? What is wrong with seeking success?

He and his wife attended the session until the end, when they returned home in silence. Alvaro contains his impressions until he arrives at his in-laws' home.

"Very well, Thereza, I've done what you wanted. That message, just so I wouldn't play the role of an imbecile, was for me?"

"Yes, dear. There was a request from the spirituality to take you there. I believe that with your presence, the spiritual entity was also present and passed the message through the medium."

"Look, Thereza, I'm not going to stop you from going to the center or doing your work. But please, I have no intention of believing what was said there, all right? Who can guarantee that this is not a fraud? Go figure!" he left, slamming the door.

She was saddened by her husband's comment. As a Spiritist, she understood that it was an act of free will on the part of her husband, and prayed that he was not being obsessed by another spirit. She would leave the matter as it was and try to continue her married life.

Criciúma, 1971 - 1996

Alvaro receives a job proposal, to leave the mining areas and work in the company's office. The proposal appears to be interesting, as it allows him to directly advice the company directors in their decision-making, and gives him greater freedom of movement, one of the requests accepted by the company. This way, he can now give consultancy to other companies; as long as they are not in the same region as the mining company, and that the travel does not exceed 5 days, three times a year.

He really was tired of working with the miners. He was aware of the suffering of the miners. After all, his father was one of them, and the imminent threat of tragedy at one point was only a matter of time. The miner's work was still very insecure. And while he was inside looking after the machines or delegating orders to his assistants, he also took the risk.

He needed to breathe fresh air, too. His son was growing up and required constant medical care, even though he was a healthy child. The doctors said he was a sensitive child. Her mood swings were perceptible by the age of four.

In 1972, Luiz was born. Physically perfect, just like his firstborn. He looked like his father, unlike Antonio Neto, who resembled his mother much more than his grandfather.

His friends said it was just a phase and that he was a first-time father. This realization made him feel more relieved. At home, the atmosphere was always one of harmony and peace, and Thereza was mainly responsible for this. He could not tell how his life would be without his lovely wife.

He bought a nice house in downtown Criciúma, left the houses in Urussanga rented, and on weekends was constructing a building in his hometown. "You never know what tomorrow will bring," he always said to himself.

The children grow up and Alvaro provides the best schools, the best doctors, and all private. With the income from his work and his estate, he hires a house cleaner for Thereza and a driver to take the children to school.

Everything seems to be flowing well, but in 1979, Antonio had a serious health crisis. Thereza was distressed; the boy seemed to be in such good health! She remembered the message she had received many years before.

The doctors ran all the tests available at the time. Nothing was found; the boy seemed to have entered a parallel world, at least during those days when he was hospitalized.

Thereza, not satisfied, calls Florianópolis to talk to a sister at the center. She tells her everything that happened, without neglecting any details.

"Your son has a very serious trauma from a previous incarnation. We must remember that many times we have been victims, and, in other incarnations, torturers. Have you ever heard of autism? Try talking to a specialist in this subject and ask to diagnose your son."

"Helena, will he be okay?" she asks, with that affliction that only mothers have.

"Yes, speak to your husband and convince him to let you bring him here when he leaves the hospital. I will try to help you. Okay?"

"Okay, Helena, I'll try to convince Alvaro."

After a few days, Antonio's condition improves. The doctors decide to discharge him, recommending the use of some medication. The boy appears to be numbed by the medicine, which mercilessly cuts into his mother's heart.

"Alvaro, what do you say you let me take him to Florianópolis? We can stay at my parents' house, who are already retired, and I can get another medical opinion on his condition."

"Honey, I think that's a great idea. I know the love you have for our son, and I totally trust your ability to find out exactly what our son's problem is. Stay as long as you need to."

She takes Antonio and Luiz to Florianópolis, in search of answers to their son's problem. Without Alvaro's suspicion, she takes Antonio to the Spiritist Center to receive passes, where he meets Helena.

"The little angel really needs you. I have been thinking about your call and got the number of Dr. André; a pediatrician specialized in autism and other issues affecting children. He is here in Florianópolis."

"Helena, you have no idea what good you do to me. I will try to schedule an appointment. I have reduced the medication and tried to interact with him as much as possible. Luiz is like his father, obedient, serious, and respects me. At eight years old, he looks like a little man."

"Call him. I have already told him about your case. He showed interest. One more piece of information that might interest you. He attends another Spiritist Center and is fully aware that the ills of the soul come from the past, or as a limitation of the present life, governed by the law of cause and effect."

That night, she sleeps peacefully. She dreams that his son is much better, happy, dedicated to a specific area of health and helping others. In the same dream, he sees Luiz, with the same greedy tendencies as his father. She wakes up feeling a little uneasy.

She tells her mother that she wants to take her son to the doctor. Having lived for many years in Urussanga, she has forgotten the names of some streets, so she asks if she knows the address.

The mother, and the grandmother, think it is more prudent to take a cab and tell him the address. She does so, arriving at the doctor's office at the appointed time.

The doctor's office really resembles a children's scenario. Toys, building blocks, crayons, a children's table, a blackboard, and other objects that are sure to calm children.

Dr. André is a docile man of African descent. He brings, from his parents, the gentleness, intelligence, and tact to deal with children. He receives Thereza in an affectionate way.

Inside the office, he interacts for an hour with Antonio, observing his responses, movements, actions, and reactions.

At the end of the diagnosis, Dr. André tells her his impressions.

"Thereza, your son is apparently autistic. His autism is average, which will not prevent him from working, developing his abilities, or interacting with other people. Autistic people observe the world differently than we do. The big secret is to try to see the world as they do."

"What would you recommend, then, on the educational side and how to treat it at home?"

"If you come from a wealthy family, hire a private teacher who is a specialist in children with psychological disorders. It will be of great value. It would be very intriguing if the selected teacher already works with autism in a proactive way, trying to encourage the child. You can bring the child here during the week or on weekends, if you want. I particularly recommend a teacher I trust for cases like yours."

"Like mine? What do you mean?" she asks, stunned.

"As incredible as it may seem, autism is much more common than you might think. The big problem is that often the diagnosis is made wrongly or late, which causes considerable damage to the child, with consequences even when adult. I believe that autism will be one of the fields that medical science will study with much more attention in the next century."

"All right, Dr. André. Let me get this straight: my son needs a teacher to help him live an almost normal life. Without someone to accompany him in the right way, the risk of him continuing in this same scenario, even as an adult, is great. Is that it?"

"That's it in a nutshell. Here is the teacher's card. Remembering that you can ask for a second opinion, of course."

"One question, Dr. André. A friend told me that you are a Spiritist. Am I correct?"

"Yes, I have attended a Spiritist Center for many years here in town."

"Interesting, I have also been a Spiritist for a long time. What work do you do in particular?"

"Thereza, I don't have any mediumistic skills, if that is the purpose of your question. I am a voracious student. I see not only the body, but the spirit that inhabits each patient. My specific function is to be a pass-giver, I transfer positive vibrations to others through my hands."

"How wonderful! My work consists of helping the center in charity work."

"Did you see how in life, nothing is by chance? Let us credit the master Jesus the opportunity of this day and your son being well taken care of by you. I always say that maternity is a remarkable honor that women possess."

"True, doctor. Thank you for your words!"

She leaves the office, with the professor's phone in hand. She takes a cab with her son again and returns to her parents' home.

"So, daughter, did you manage to talk to the doctor?"

"Yes, mom. Antonio has autism, but it is treatable and can be reversed in his favor."

"Oh, that's great, daughter! I love my grandchildren and you can count on us to help them. How will you handle this situation with Alvaro?"

"Mom, I can handle him. I do not think I will have any problems spending some time here. He only lives for work. Work and money, money and work."

"Is your marriage having difficulties?"

"Not yet, Mom. However, if he continues at this pace and stops taking care of us, maybe so. Alvaro has always been a good man, you know that."

"Yes, I know, daughter. Well, let's wait until tomorrow and you can go back home in your father's car, since you came by bus with the children. What do you think? Leave the children with us!"

"Mom, you don't have the energy to put up with two mischievous grandchildren…"

"Not at all, my child. You do not know the powers of grandparents."

"Okay, Mom. I will go back to Criciúma tomorrow."

She sleeps with the children in the guest room because the bed is big. They both sleep peacefully; while she worries that for a while, it will be necessary for Antonio to remain periodically in Florianópolis for treatment.

When she wakes up, she calls the teacher and schedules an appointment. The teacher informs her that she can help him at home, since this is the way she usually helps her students. So, she tells the teacher the address of her parents' home.

She receives her at the scheduled time and introduces Antonio so that they can exchange impressions. After two hours, she seems to interact very well with him.

"Mom, can I give you a suggestion? Isn't there an APFE in the city of Criciúma?"

"APFE?"

"Yes, the Association of Parents and Friends of the Exceptional. Do you know it?"

"Yes, I've heard of it."

"Then, I recommend the work of the professionals at APFE. He can live with his family and eventually, I can accompany him on Fridays. What do you think?"

"I think it's a great idea!"

The teacher really makes an impression on Helena. She seems to be dedicated and sincere about the idea of enrolling Antonio in APFE. She had heard that everyone who participates in the association is a good person with an incredible love for all children.

She then returns to Criciúma and explains the whole picture to Alvaro.

"Honey, our son is not retarded!"

"Alvaro, APFE is a wonderful place for children with special needs, whether physical or psychological. The one here is great, ask your colleagues!"

"Very good, Ms. Know-it-all. Let us do a test. Let him stay there for three months. If he does not make progress, I will hire this teacher on an exclusive basis. Are we clear?"

Age was not doing Alvaro any good. He was becoming an arrogant person with a difficult temper. The feeling of empathy seems to have disappeared, believing that money buys everything.

Bruna studied architecture, graduated and lives in the north of the state. She is happy and well, recently married to a good man, a physical education teacher. They are planning to have children and love their nephews and nieces.

Antonio's progress at APFE Criciúma is remarkable. The teachers have understood that his autism is treatable and have sought to extend his positive abilities. In 1984, the teachers discharged him. He is very intelligent and can interact with other people. His IQ test, gave above average.

He manages to learn to read and write, and is very curious about medical subjects, even passing with honors the entrance exam for high school convalidation.

In 1985, he applied to the Medical School entrance exam. Although he is shy and extremely logical, he gets an excellent grade and is admitted to the UFSC. He goes to live with his grandparents, who disincarnate in 1989 and 1990, respectively.

In 1990, he graduates from UFSC with a medical degree, with a monograph on autism and new approaches to treatment. He begins to practice in partnership with his former teacher and Dr. André, who is about to retire.

Starting in 1992, Luiz helps his father run the family business. The rentals, the purchase of new properties, and the initial work to structure a new construction company in the coal region. Like his father, he is obstinate, but thanks to his mother's work, he does not see money as an objective in life. He learned from her that charity can be done selflessly, and took over the management of the business in 1996, with his father's retirement.

The two brothers live peacefully, eventually one frequenting the other's home. Luiz married a girl from Urussanga and has a son, Eduardo.

With Eduardo's arrival, there was a sort of softening in Alvaro's heart. It seems that, initially, the birth of his grandchild made him reflect on life. A small spark that life is more than just the accumulation of wealth.

He spends long afternoons with his grandson, like every first-time grandfather. He observes that not even his father was healthy enough or had enough time to have the plenitude of more direct contact like the one he has with his grandson.

He was fifty-three years old, with two children, an amazing woman and a good grandchild. What more could he want in life? What did life need to teach him?

He kept thinking of these issues. And Thereza had been participating in the local Spiritist Centers for years, maintaining the same kindness and patience as always.

The Accident, 1997

Coming from Florianópolis to Criciúma by car at night. It was Thursday, a rainy winter day. The black VW Santana was new. As he was about to pass a car, on the famous straight in Imbituba, he saw the headlights of a blue Mercedes-Benz in front of him. His reflexes only give him time to throw the car off the track, crashing heavily into a tree.

He wakes up hours later in the hospital. When he opens his eyes, he seems to be fine. However, as he is opening his eyes, he realizes that something is wrong. His arms are bandaged. A tube comes out of his ribs. His legs are immobilized. He cannot speak; he has a tube in his mouth.

He blinks several times to the nurse. She notices and calls the doctor.

"Doctor, he's awake!"

"Well, it's a miracle he's alive and came out of the coma so quickly. Really, it is a miracle."

"Thanks to St. Camillus!" says the nurse.

"Tell the woman in the waiting room that he's awake, please." Said the doctor.

"Right away, doctor."

She immediately goes to the waiting room to give notice.

"Mrs. Thereza, your husband is awake. The doctor will run some tests to see if he can communicate and I'll call you, okay?"

"Of course, what a relief to know he's alive!" says Thereza, accompanied by her two children.

She goes back to the ICU (Intensive Care Unit).

"Doctor, is he lucid?"

"That's what we're going to find out now… Can you hear me? If so, blink twice."

Alvaro listens to everything and blinks twice.

"Very good! Now, try to squeeze my finger with your right hand, the one I am making an X with the pen."

He tries, he tries, but he cannot.

"It's okay, Mr. Alvaro. There is nothing to worry about. Now, let us do a sensitivity test. I am going to put a pen on your feet, and the nurse will be watching you. If you feel anything, wink, all right?"

He blinks twice, confirming that you understand.

The doctor rubs the pen on his feet and he feels nothing. He gets worried.

"Nothing? Answer by blinking twice if you didn't feel anything."

He blinks twice.

"Now let's go to the left arm. I will do the X and if you feel it, blink twice. In this arm, you felt nothing. Now the hands."

Nothing, he thought. Nothing at all. Have I become a quadriplegic or paraplegic?

"Mr. Alvaro, you will leave the ICU and remain under observation for a few days, maybe a week or more. The neurological tests did not show any cranial trauma, which in your case is a great victory. I explained the situation to your doctor son, and while you were in the coma, he accompanied me and helped me with the procedures, he is an excellent professional. It is he who can help you at first, for the moment. Tomorrow I will visit you and let your family members visit you."

Thereza enters the ICU with her children and sees her husband. She passes her hands over his face and, so moved, cries. He cannot speak! How he didn't appreciate the fact that he could walk or do his activities so naturally!

"Darling, you'll be fine. God has protected you. Now, rest and let's concentrate our faith and prayers on your recovery. All right?"

"Madam, since he can't speak, he is communicating with the blink of an eye. If he understands, blinks twice, okay?" says the nurse, who accompanies them.

"Yes, I understand. Do you understand, my love?"

He blinks twice.

"Good. When can he be discharged?"

"In a few days or a week. We will transfer him to a room and wait for his clinical evolution."

"Thank you, doctor!"

He is moved to a room, where he receives all the necessary medical treatment. The tube is removed and he can breathe normally, but not the bandages.

He tries to speak, but still cannot. During his next visits, the doctor informs him that he will bring in a speech therapist to help him regain his speech. He nods positively.

Five days later, the speech therapist arrives.

"Mr. Alvaro, we're going to try to get you to talk, okay? You must be patient and not make any more effort than necessary. Is that okay?"

Two blinks.

"Let's try to speak the A word. Try to pull the air into your lungs. Can you do it?"

Two blinks.

"Now push the air out, trying to get it through the roof of your mouth."

"AAAAH"

"Very good! Congratulations, this is the best news of the day. Starting today, for one hour a day, we will speak all the letters and numbers of the alphabet."

During the days in which he stayed at the hospital, he was able to speak all the letters of the alphabet and numbers.

The doctors call Thereza and sons.

"The situation is as follows. He was quadriplegic initially, but I believe he can regain movement, but not leg movement. You can try to get other opinions, but I believe they will come to the same consensus. Your son understood what I was talking about when I showed him the tests. We will discharge him, but he will need physical and speech therapy, as well as a nurse. He will still need to keep his cast on for quite a while longer. As far as I know, you can afford to keep him at home. Do you all agree?"

"Yes, we agree. Maybe the domestic air and the contact with my son will help him," says Luiz.

An ambulance then transports him to Criciúma, directly to his home. A hospital bed and professionals were brought in.

Only after three months, he was able to remove the casts and articulate words. In the meantime, he was able to move his arms and hands, confirming the initial diagnosis of the doctors who attended him. In the following months, he gradually recovered his movements, except for his legs. He was paraplegic.

For a long time, he was sad and depressed. His wife eventually talked about God, but his mind still insisted on rationalism.

The accident, according to him, was a mere miscalculation when overtaking and his survival was due to the fact that the car was already going a little slower.

His grandson is his constant companion, as well as his wife. Thereza, always her! What would he be without her?

Thereza's disincarnation, 2000

Thereza was at home when she suddenly felt ill and fainted almost immediately. She had suffered a hemorrhagic stroke. He was at home, but in another room, in his wheelchair. Five minutes later, when he changes rooms, he sees his wife lying there.

"Thereza! Thereza! Oh, my God!" he says, helpless with the situation.

He calls the fire department, which arrives quickly. They take her to the hospital and he asks their private driver to take him with them.

"Come on, Hugo, take me to the hospital."

"Calm down, sir. We'll be there soon."

At the private hospital, he arrives at the information desk. He asks for his wife. The attendant dials an extension. After a few minutes, the general practitioner arrives.

"You are her husband, right?"

"Yes, I am. What happened, a heart attack?"

"No, there was a massive hemorrhagic stroke. She is in the ICU, in a coma. We are trying to do everything possible to stabilize her at this early stage."

"Doctor, is there any way I can wait here?"

"Yes, if your health insurance has some coverage for an accompanying person, you can reserve a room."

"All right, I'll do that, thank you."

In a coma, she saw herself in a truly green, calm, windless place. She sees some family members who have been disincarnated for some time.

"Dear, you are in a coma, on Earth. That is why the spiritual bonds are thinner. It is very possible that you will disincarnate, but your mission before your children and husband is accomplished. You are worthy of even passing through the Umbral. There are spiritual friends around you, on the physical plane."

"But what about Alvaro? How will he be? He won't live without me!"

"He will live, dear. Or, have you forgotten that life always goes on?"

"I have never forgotten, the doctrine has always clarified that life goes on!"

"So, here we are."

"But what brings me to disincarnate now?"

"Alvaro needs to change his attitudes and thought patterns. And anyway, the mission that you yourself assumed before incarnating has been completed."

"I will miss my family members so much!"

"Don't worry, God never deserts us, those we love only move away from us temporarily. We are eternal spirits!"

Thereza spent three weeks in the ICU, and disincarnated that Saturday morning. When Alvaro found out, it seemed as if his world was going to collapse. Nothing would make sense anymore. He did not care if he was in a wheelchair, but he really wanted her by his side.

The funeral processions were done as she had asked, while she was still alive. Her Spiritist friends were there, since death is a natural stage in eternal life, and they all remembered the good moments, sending positive vibrations to her, who was in a deep sleep in a spiritual colony.

Alvaro spent the following years in a deep bitterness, only dispersed by the constant presence of his grandson, who was growing and bringing with him much love and patience for his grandfather. Bruna, too, visited her brother often, bringing her daughter Maria to see her uncle.

Alvaro was no longer the same man, he lived longing of the past. Some friends asked him if he would like to go to a church or even a Spiritist Center.

He refused, saying that he would never change the concept that he was a rational man.

His children also made gestures of faith and peace to their father, inviting him to practice charity or good deeds. He said that he already did good by employing numerous people. For him, this was a way of doing good, putting food on people's tables.

To bear the loss of his wife, he went back to active work. He adapted, in the construction company's headquarters, a ramp to go up and down, doors and tables to attend meetings. Energetic, not accepting postponements or excuses, many felt that Alvaro was too demanding. Some former employees resigned, and new ones were hired, with a thirst for power and money.

Alvaro manipulated them, playing a game of who was better than the other, only to bring the results he expected. He fired and hired without any empathy, based solely on numbers.

His sons thought it was better not to interfere with their father's activities, including Luiz, who could be more sagacious than his father could, remembered his mother's words, that free-will decides everything, besides divine providence.

Cancer, 2006

For some time now, he had a nagging, lacerating headache. He took painkillers and the pain went away. On a certain day, he took the medicine and the pain did not go away. Another day, the same thing.

He lived with the throbbing pain for two days, when he decided to see a neurologist.

"Doctor, I have a very annoying headache that hasn't gone away for days."

"May be a migraine, but let's do some general tests, and a CT scan, okay?"

"Of course, no problem. And how can we make the pain go away, at least for now?"

"I'm going to give you a stronger painkiller."

He took the stronger medication and it did work. He scheduled all the exams with the doctor and he called Alvaro the following week.

"Mr. Alvaro, I would like you to come back. Is there a family member that can accompany you?"

"Yes, my son."

"Very good, come on Wednesday at 9:00 PM."

The surgeon, very well known in the southern region of the state, was famous for being an excellent diagnostician, and it was difficult for a second opinion to go against his.

He enters the room, accompanied by his son Luiz.

"Mr. Alvaro, we have a problem. A glioma is cuasing your headache."

"Glioma?"

"Yes, a brain cancer that still challenges us nowadays. It is complex to define where the healthy brain ends and the affected part."

The news hits his son like a bomb, but Alvaro continues to reason logically.

"Very well, is there a surgery?"

"Yes, it's risky, but your glioma has already taken a considerable part of your brain. If it is well removed, you will have a few more years of overtime."

"Overtime?"

"Yes, of course. A significant portion of brain operations is aimed at ensuring the patient's overtime. Are you a logical person?"

"Of course!"

"So, you understand what I'm trying to tell you, right?"

"Yes, you are saying that I have cancer of a type that is difficult to operate on and if the operation is successful, I have some extra time. Obviously, you are going to ask me if I want to have the surgery."

"Obviously. If you wish, I will do it as soon as possible."

"Very well, I know that in order to perform these surgeries, I have to sign a risk contract. Just give me the contract to read and let's get down to the facts."

"No problem, but the surgery is only done with a signed contract. It's at your own risk, I assume you know that."

"I do know that. I just want to discuss it with my son."

"Is your son a lawyer?"

"This one is a business administrator. The other one is a doctor."

"Take a copy, please."

"Thank you, doctor."

"At your service."

"Should I keep taking the painkiller?"

"Yes, but don't increase the dose."

Goes home. His son talks to him, still very shocked.

"Dad, you're sick and you weren't afraid?"

"My son, I am rational. Is everything okay with you? I am sick, I like to live, and some extra time is not bad at all. The doctor is good, but there is no satisfaction guaranteed or some institution to complain about after the grave, is there? I just want to talk to your brother."

"Do you want a second opinion?"

"When you hire the best, there is no second opinion, my son. I want to understand the process of the surgery, in case your brother knows, that's all. With this internet thing, it is very possible to have a video call, right? Like these satellite TVs, right?"

"Yes, we can use Skype.

"Does your brother have this thing?

"Of course, Dad, it's the 2000s.

"Then make sure I can talk to him."

The next day, in the evening, Alvaro speaks with Antonio.

"Hey son, how are you? Since I already know you, your brother must have told you everything. As I'm not a man of half-words or actions, can you explain to me how this surgery works?"

"Father, there are two ways. Through a camera, where the surgeon identifies and removes the area, through an orifice, if it is small or if it is extensive, in the popular jargon, they open your head. The advantage of being an open surgery is the better identification of the extension of the cancer."

"How is the post-operative period?"

"It depends; we don't know what sequels will be left or if you will become disabled. Maybe nothing will happen, but you cannot measure the risks. Cancer is cancer."

"Let's imagine that I come out well. What is the subsequent treatment?"

"Radio and chemotherapy, depending on the treatment."

"What about quality of life?"

"In your case, possibly quite depreciated."

"Thank you, son, that's what I wanted to hear. Do you recommend surgery?"

"Based on the reports I've seen, if you don't have the surgery, you will have only months to live. If you do, you may have between one and many more years. As a doctor, I recommend the surgery, even though you are my father."

"Luiz?"

"Yes."

"Schedule the surgery."

Two weeks later, the surgery was being performed. The adopted method was the open modality, with Alvaro totally sedated. After a few hours, he awoke from his anesthetic sleep. It seems he had survived. There he was, years later, in an ICU.

The doctor did tests similar to the accident and found that it is normal in some cases to take a while to regain sensation in some limbs.

He stayed in the ICU for four days, with daily monitoring by the surgeon. In the room, he received all the necessary treatment and was released fifteen days later, without feeling his right arm yet.

At the doctor's office, he was updated on the results of the surgery.

"Mr. Alvaro, I have good news: we have removed practically the entire tumor. Nevertheless, since it is a glioma, we will be careful and apply radio and chemotherapy so that it does not come back, and if it does, not so quickly. The bad news is that unfortunately your right arm is paralyzed because of the glioma itself. Do you understand? The other functions are normal, which is a great relief in a case like this."

"What additional recommendations can you give us?" asked Luiz.

"Honestly, if your father is working, even retired, I recommend total rest. Subsequent therapies exhaust the patient. That's it for today, and we'll schedule the therapy sessions as soon as possible."

Alvaro did all the chemo and radiotherapy sessions until the beginning of 2007.

He endured the side effects of the therapies with resilience, but there were other surprises to come.

Metastasis and disincarnation, 2007

The headache was back. He had found it strange, after all the treatment he had received. Maybe it was an adverse effect of the medication. He called the doctor and asked for another consultation, which was promptly attended to.

Examinations were made and again, the doctor requested the presence of a son. Alvaro automatically understood that good news were not on the horizon.

"We have a suspected return of the glioma. However, this time I recommend we do a PET Scan, which is an exam that analyzes the body thoroughly in search of new tumors. Do you agree?"

"Of course, no problem."

The exam was done, revealing metastasis in other parts of the body. When they returned from the exam, an oncologist trusted by the neurosurgeon was accompanying them.

"Mr. Alvaro, I'm bringing this time Dr. Alexandre, oncologist. The exam showed metastasis in other areas. This time, I do not recommend another surgery. We do not know exactly which area it will affect. From now on, you can do palliative treatments."

"You mean live on pain medication, is that it?"

"Yes, that's basically it."

"How long do I have left?"

"We do not like to give out this information, but in your case, at most one year to live."

"Does chemo and radio help?"

"Yes, for you to reach this one year of life, it is necessary for you to undergo these treatments, mainly because of the metastasis in some organs."

"Thank you for your sincerity."

"You are welcome."

He leaves the room with his son, this time upset. Now it was the end of the line. However, looking back, there was nothing to complain about. Good children, grandson, admirable wife. Accomplished parents, what more did he want?

Thereza would say that he should take advantage of this time and accept God and Jesus. Even though he was sick, the idea still did not convince him.

One afternoon in 2007, he felt very ill at home. He had just enough time to call the maid. He had a massive heart attack and collapsed under his wheelchair.

Umbral, 2007 - 2017

In a flashback of his life, perhaps he began to remember what he had missed in his life: helping others. The long days, which were lost in the reckoning, began to create a logic in Alvaro's spirit.

In all these years he had been beaten, assaulted, drank swamp water, and in his terrifying desperation, he cried out to God. But to cry out for divine help, one had to believe in Him. He remembered the Bible, the fact that his father had faith, with his father in his speeches saying that "without faith you can't go far, and that God exists", just as his mother had the same conviction.

Not to mention the most concrete example, which was Thereza. Thereza always tried in every way to make him believe in God. If he is there in that place, fetid, with horrible beings, then he was wrong somewhere. Was it the lack of faith in God or not doing good? Or both?

As the days and years went by, he began to walk through the regions of the Umbral. Recalling all his past life, he remembered that one of those who had received him how much time had passed, for there was no calendar or night, somehow said that "someone" had rescued him from there in his previous life. Who was this someone?

He began every day (he realized that the interval of days, what he assumed, was the decrease in light in the Umbral for certain hours) to pray and ask God to light his path and bring him faith. And to have mercy on him by taking him to a better place.

Ten years passed, but he did not know it. On one of these days, his mother visits him in the Umbral.

"Mother? What are you doing here and so much younger?"

"I came to see you, my son. I asked the higher beings a lot for the possibility of seeing you."

"Mother, how do I get out of here?"

"With faith, my son, with faith. God is merciful, but you must believe in Him and in Jesus."

"Dear mother, with all the desolation that I see here and with all the headache I have felt for years, it is impossible not to believe that God and Jesus exist anymore! Have you come to pick me up?"

"No, dear, the higher spirits are the ones who decide the time. But I am very happy that you are already accepting Jesus and God the Father. Continue praying because I will continue in the spiritual colony praying for you. I love you, my son."

"Mom, can someone visit me again?"

"If you are deserving, maybe so. Stay with God, my son."

She leaves, and he is immensely happy. So, it's true, there is such a thing as life after death. Even more reason to believe everything she said. And Thereza, her father, how are they? He misses these two, they were good to him, and now he understands that he could have been a much better son and husband.

In a numb, almost sleepy state, he sees two men carrying a stretcher.

They then walk up to him. One of the men touches him and calls him by name.

"Alvaro?"

"Yes, it's me."

"Come with us."

The umbral spirits observe the situation, and some of them exalt feelings of anger and hatred against those two men dressed in white. As if Alvaro, and all the others, were their property. He had been rescued.

He went into a deep sleep as he was carried by the stretcher. He didn't know it, but he was being taken to the Spiritual Colony called the Colony of Flowers, for a long treatment.

At the same time, he had not even realized that ten earthly years had passed. He had not seen his funeral or burial because in spirituality "each disincarnation is a disincarnation".

At this very moment, on the earth plane, the grandson was praying to his beloved grandfather before going to sleep.

"Lord God the Father, Jesus, beloved brother. Take care of the spirit of our disincarnate ones, especially of my grandfather Alvaro. Give us also the discernment to do good and the detachment from everything that is transitory. Amen."

The Colony of Flowers

He woke up with a stranger next to him. The place was white, clean, and with a window that allowed them to see a tree. It was a very cozy place. The headache was still there, but less intense. In fact, much less. It seemed much more like a memory of all the time he had been in that horrid place, than the cancer that afflicted him.

He was also wearing clean clothes, smelling good. Someone had bathed his body.

"Alvaro, you are in the colony of flowers, which is in the region of Santa Catarina and Paraná. Welcome!"

"Thank you! How can I thank those who brought me here?"

"They don't need gratitude. The work of helping the spirits has been already the payment for their work."

"Your name, what would it be?"

"Hermes."

"Very well, Hermes. Apart from this headache, I feel fine. Everything seems to be working, can I help you with something here?"

"Hum… yes. However, one thing at a time. I think it is important to clarify a few things before anything else. You are here thanks to some incarnate and disincarnate people, besides spending ten earthly years in the Umbral, which is not a long time, if you take into account that your spirit is eternal."

"All right, I get it. But how can I know how I ended up there, if I haven't done anything wrong?"

"Dear Alvaro, didn't you ever hear on Earth that the fact of not doing good is already a certain way of doing evil?"

"Of course, of course, the Orientals talk about it a lot. My wife used to talk about it too. Ah, I think I understand. I ended up there for not doing good, is that it? However, I wasn't a bandit or anything like that."

"Calm down, calm down. I think the answer is more or less in your words. I will not be the one to answer it, and it will be answered in due course. Are you a patient spirit?"

"After having passed through that place, I believe so."

"Very well, you will rest for a few days and then we will speak again. Perhaps other spirits will visit you, and a nurse will give you permission to visit the garden."

He rethought about life for a few days. There was day and night there, and it seemed that the disincarnated people moved less, or even rested.

Another day, another stranger.

"Good morning! Have you eaten the food that was on the table?"

"Yes, but it didn't look like food, but I assumed it was to be eaten."

"Very well, now let's go out into the garden."

He calmly got up and went with the stranger to the garden. There were many people, none of them familiar. The only resemblance was their features, very similar to those of the incarnates in the area where he lived. Other than that, nothing else. The environment was always clean, the spirits were always calm, and they talked to each other.

"Later on you should attend a lecture, which we call a reintroduction to the spirit world lecture. When you get to the end of the garden, you will see a large dome. It is there."

"Do these lectures take place every day?"

"Yes, you have no idea how many disincarnates we receive."

"Oh, good! At least they are well here."

"That's right, thank you for the good thought."

He calmly goes to the large dome and sits in the last row, as his grandmother used to teach him that in temples, you always sit in the last row.

A young man goes to a higher part, much like an altar, without a microphone.

"Dear brothers and sisters. You have recently been welcomed here, in the Colony of the Flowers. Each one of you had explicit reasons for being in the Umbral, from where you were gathered at different points in time. When I say time, I mean earthly time, which does not exist here, it is only a measure until your spirit gets used to the air of eternity. As you can attest, the spirit is eternal and God is merciful. Many of you are here through the intercession of disincarnate family members, others through the prayers of acquaintances, and many others through the selfless prayers of strangers. I want to tell you that all of you, in due course, will get the answers you need. I recommend to all of you, if so requested by the coordinating spirits, to try to perform proactive tasks. An active spirit, for the benefit of others, continually evolves for its own sake. Thank you very much, and see you soon!"

Some spirits are lost and in doubt, and seek to talk to some people. A woman approaches him.

"Don't you think it's good to be here? I slept on earth and woke up here. Can you believe that we are eternal?"

"My Lady, of this I am certain, but as for any other questions you might want to ask me, I am not the right person. I am still confused about many things and I am grateful to be here."

"Were you somewhere else?"

"Yes, I was in the Umbral for a long time. I would very much like to know where I went wrong, how I went wrong and how to try not to go wrong anymore, maybe I can see my wife and children again, as well as my parents."

"Were you a bad person?"

"No, no. I was an engineer, I had a family, an ordinary man, possibly too greedy over the years and possibly not doing good. And you, what did you do there?"

"I was prime minister of the Catholic Church. It took me a while to believe that I was still alive. I mean, we are always led to believe that there is only heaven and hell and you only live once. I think it's a little different," she says, giggling.

"And you, were you, shall we say, practicing good?

"Oh yes, my good friend. I helped people a lot. I liked to help and I was always much attached to God, Jesus and family values."

"And you came from there to here, for what reason?"

"I think it was a natural death. I was waking up and passed out. So, I woke up here. And you?"

"Brain cancer."

"You must have suffered a quite a bit!"

"We can say so, but I think this part also has an explanation. It seems that somehow, I'm connecting the dots."

"I think that somehow, when we are here, we all end up connecting the dots. Have you been to any other lectures?"

"No, not yet. And you?"

"My first one, too. Would you mind keeping me company until we find someone who can help us in some way?"

"Of course, now that we possibly have time, let's go seek someone who can help us."

Walking through the garden, they notice that there is a man who guides the spirits. They go there.

“Sir, can you help us?”

“Of course.”

“We want to know why we are here, especially my friend here, who needs more answers than I do. Is there someone who can guide us?”

“There is, but as you can see, there are many spirits in similar situations to yours. When the time is right, someone will come looking for you.”

“Thank you!”

“It’s a pity we don’t have any answers, I would like some!” she says, walking with Alvaro.

“Me too, but patience is needed. I think this is a virtue we have to learn here. That is a fact!”

“Well Madam, I must go, I prefer not to disrespect rules, much less return to that place. If you excuse me, I would like to go back and find my place of rest and meditation. If I am wanted, it will possibly be there. Thank you!”

“A pleasure, gentleman!

He walks until he finds the building where he is resting. He remembers the corridor: 3A and room 328. He goes back to the place and lies down again.

Hours go by, he rambles on about how his earthly life could have been better. In a kind of dream, he sees himself in other lives. As an evil, ruthless, sordid man. He wakes up worried. Was that he in a past life?

Sometime later, Hermes appears again.

"Alvaro, positive impressions of the Colony?"

"All possible and unimaginable. I discovered some interesting things, such as the need to practice patience. At the same time, I would like to know how I thank God for the opportunity to be here."

"In the same way that we do on earth or in other orbs: through prayer. No matter the language, God, Jesus, and the higher spirits interpret the real feeling of our spirit."

"Very good, it's just that I hardly ever did that on Earth, you know?"

"Yes, I do, I receive a record from the disincarnate spirits that I assist."

"Oh, really?"

"Of course, if you notice, there is no sign here with your name, and how I called you Alvaro?"

"Telepathy?"

"It could be, but my spiritual level is not much different from yours. I have just been here longer and have been assigned tasks, just as you will soon be assigned tasks that will become more and more complex with time, until the arrival of your reincarnation."

"Reincarnation?"

"Of course! Spiritual life is much greater than life in orbs. Life on earth, for example, is a field of trials and expiation. When we evolve, we go to regeneration orbs, where violence and inequality are almost non-existent, and where there is much more empathy among people."

"Is that right?"

"Of course, of course! I see that you still do not remember at all the other passages in other colonies..."

"Other colonies?" he asks, surprised.

"Of course, but I still assume that you are under the effect of the veil of oblivion. As you change your spiritual vibration, it is slowly broken."

"Do you mean that I have had other lives?"

"Other lives, in different bodies, other planets, and in adverse situations to the current one."

"Oh, my goodness!" he says surprised.

"Your concern did not impress me. Before, yes, I arrived just like you. I was rescued by the selfless prayers of some unknown incarnate spirits. There are legions of people who pray in cemeteries, churches or other places. All the people glow with faith, and many of them say prayers on behalf of the forgotten. And I was one of them, I was there for a long time in the Umbral."

"Was it difficult for you?" the curiosity in Alvaro is more and more latent.

"Yes, of course. Let's say that, like you, I didn't know how to enjoy my earthly life and I accumulated some debts."

"Debts? What would be debts?"

"More actions to repair, besides those that were already in my incarnational plan."

"You don't say! But most people on Earth always commit faults."

"That's true. That is why this and other colonies exist, and why rarely does anyone come directly here. Only if it is a person who has practiced a lot of charity, or has paid off their debt from that incarnational plane in full, something that is difficult."

"So everyone goes to that place where I was?"

"Well, that's just one of the places. Let us say that the Umbral is defined in levels. You were neither in the least bad nor the worst, you were in the middle. The lower the vibration of the place, the less light and more density you perceive, plus the unpleasant smells and creatures."

"Will that place ever be empty?"

"No, because God always, in time, creates spirits."

"Creates life, then?"

"Let's say yes, for your understanding."

"I'm asking too many questions, right?"

"No, absolutely normal questions."

"Will I return to Earth then?"

"Sincerely, I can't tell you. The Earth will be transformed, and those who do not pass the year, let us say, will reincarnate on another lower planet."

"But isn't this a kind of punishment or retrogression?"

"The spirit never retrogresses. It only stagnates. God, in His merciful justice, allows advanced spirits for that orb to incarnate there as a test, and at the same time as an element of progress in that world."

"Earth seems to me to be a reasonably good planet."

"Actually, it is, but the incarnated spirits that live there, almost all of them are in trials or expiation."

"Trials, expiation?"

"Yes, trials is when they, themselves, before reincarnating, decide by themselves, which challenge they want to go through. Depending on their free will choice, they end up going through the trial, succumbing or successfully completing it, eliminating their debt. And expiation is when divine justice imposes that situation on you, for the purpose of experiencing the situation and having the chance of remission with it."

"Hum, interesting! So, I assume that possibly I have had a life as an incarnate, in the form of a trial."

"From the basic information I got from your file, presumably yes. Now you will need to account for the benefit not fully absorbed, shall we say?"

"Eh?"

"Yes, but it won't be me who will tell you about it. It will be another spirit, usually after some time. Everyone here is educated, everyone here is reincarnated somewhere in the universe."

"All right. Hermes. Thank you and apologies for taking your time."

"Time is what we have most here, nice to talk to you again!"

"Do you have some work for me?"

"Let's see if we can find something, it's good for the spirit."

Time goes by, until the day that he stays for hours in the garden, talking to other spirits. He asks many questions, answers theirs, but still remembers nothing of his past. It is like the life of a pensioner in a retirement home, —he compares.

Sometime later, he doesn't know exactly how long, a man appears in his room.

"Alvaro?"

"Yes, that's me."

"We have a job for you."

"Good, then let's go right now!"

"Don't you want to know what it's about?"

"I don't care, you are going to help someone, either spirit or incarnate, aren't you?"

"Yes, yes. Who would believe it!, Alvaro."

The two of them leave for the creek, which provides magnetized fluids for the new arrivals, and for the spirits who have already stayed longer.

"Your task is to filter the water. You can see that there are some leaves that fall into the water and it is not interesting to drink it with the leaf, right?"

"Yes, but with a machine, we could solve this!" he says, thinking like an engineer.

"Alvaro, if you look around, we only use technology for certain situations. All technology that encourages leisure, such as smartphones on Earth, does not exist here. That's why you are going to do an outstanding job, removing the leaves on the small side around the creek."

"I get it."

"You only finish your work when another spirit appears, okay?"

"Great."

He then works very hard and willingly on the task, no matter how simple it may be. This made him reflect that he did not give his employees the importance they deserved, did not wish them good morning, and did not treat them in the best possible way. Time went by without him noticing, until a young woman appeared at his side.

"I think your work is finished for today."

"Yes, will you continue?"

"Exactly, you are now my new assistant. Now, half of the time I have been here, I have been assigned to another task."

"Thank you!"

"No problem!"

He returns to his room, and stands looking out the window at the small tree. It really does look like autumn, as if it were on Earth; otherwise, the leaves would not be falling. When will his relatives make contact?

On the other days, until they call him for his daily task, he tries to help other spirits in his own resting place. He organizes the clothes of the newly arrived disincarnates, throwing them away, visits other rooms, talking to other people, when there is someone accompanying him and if he is allowed to.

Gradually, he realizes that his conscience is his great judge. Of course, God also has his way of judging acts and actions, but in a rudimentary way, this is the realization he has so far.

Months go by until a very handsome gentleman, of African origin, introduces himself to him in his room.

"Mr. Alvaro?" the spirit asks.

"Yes."

"The time has come for you to find out why you are here, and the faults of your last incarnation. Are you interested in knowing them?"

"Of course, I think that's why we are here. To perfect ourselves."

"I think you have learned quickly. As always…"

"What do you mean, as always?"

"Come with me, please."

They then move to a large room, with technological equipment still unknown to him. Everything is three-dimensional or holographic.

"This is what we call the database of past lives. Many are authorized to access only the last life, the more evolved can access even more because spiritual preparation is required to access certain contents. You have been allowed to see the last incarnation, that is, this one in which you are called Alvaro. Can we see it? I must remind you of the Biblical phrase 'all that which is hidden will be revealed'. Do you accept?"

"Yes, yes, I need to know my faults."

Several scenes from his life are played in the form of a hologram. He sees himself in the most varied situations in life, from childhood until the moment of disincarnation. He realizes that there are various key moments, whether alone, with his parents, with his sister or Thereza, as well as his children.

The spirit pauses the visualization.

"Questions?"

"There are many, but it's better to ask the useful ones. As I understand it, I was wrong in not doing good, is that correct?"

"Yes, this is one of your mistakes."

"Can you point out the others?"

"Of course. You did not believe in God until the moment you were in the worst of suffering. For some reason your rationality, that which worked against moral evolution, began to work in your favor. You also mistreated several people, you were selfish, miserly, and you were a rich man that could have helped several people. You saw materialism as an end in life activity, which is totally repudiating before the divine laws."

"I am totally guilty of these actions. And what is the role of Thereza and my children, besides my parents?"

"The family nucleus, when solid in different incarnations, can separate for a certain time, but not eternally. Love never separates, it always unites, and you must remember that the spirit is eternal. Thereza is a superior spirit, so much so that the information I got when I was asked to study your case is precisely that Thereza was under no obligation to be your wife and mother to your son, and yet she was. Your oldest son, who is still incarnated, Antonio, was one of the tests for you to break your heart and seek divine charity and faith. This did not happen. Your son Luiz, is a lure from a previous life. You had another type of connection, in some negative way. And your parents, you came to them as proof and expiation for you."

"What do you mean, expiation for me, in the case of my parents?"

"In a very previous life, you did them a lot of harm. Have you ever heard the maxim that a spirit must pay back every last cent of what he owes? Then, the mercy of God is like a patient collector. The debt can be postponed, but must be paid. With them, you proceeded very well, especially through the veil of oblivion. For them, it was a proof, that there was a harmonious coexistence. It is to your credit that you were also zealous with your sister Bruna. If you had the same care for other people, it is very possible that you would not have passed through the Umbral and would have disincarnated naturally, and perhaps you would not have had the accident."

"What do you mean?"

"The law of cause and effect can operate on the earthly plane. As I told you, God is very just. You lived for many years focused on materialism. The Superior Spirituality gave you a moratorium after the accident so that you could change through what we call inner reform, that is, the change of actions and vibrational frame. The cancer was the purge of the spirit in the body, of the negative vibrations and actions that you had."

"I got it. One last question, do I have many debts?"

"Yes, but because of your moral advancement, you are not allowed to access them yet. You will pay them unconsciously, but I can tell you that you have had at least ten incarnations on planet Earth, and in most of them, you have failed. Always through the mercy or intercession of previous relatives, you have the opportunity to reincarnate. And you often fail, as do most of the incarnates on earth."

"So that's why you said that I always learn fast..."

"Yes, in the last 500 earth years, we have had this same conversation three times."

"Was there a difference between them, the conversations?"

"Yes, it was in different colonies and this time, there is sincere interest in practicing charity. Which was not visible in the times we met. You were extremely materialistic, and had to go through situations of extreme poverty and early disincarnation, in order to break this sequence of vicissitudes. Now it seems that at least this goal has been or can be broken. We will only know for sure in the next incarnation."

"Will I incarnate on Earth?"

"No, but you will find other spirits incarnated there, with the same affinity, as well as others of a different vibratory nature. I hope you succeed in your next reincarnation because the moral success of it will be very important for your evolution."

"Good, I'm glad. I hope these impressions are not lost in the veil of oblivion."

"Me too, dear friend. I wish you success. However, you will still spend some years here in this colony, as a selfless collaborator. The Earth will go through pandemic events, other scourges, and your work will be of vital importance because all the good you do, advocates everywhere for your spirit."

"Thank you, I feel very good here! May I find my family members from the current incarnation? I miss them."

"When the time is right, you will be granted this benefit. Peace and light! Stay with God and Jesus!"

Reunions

He had stopped keeping track of time. The work in the colony was very rewarding and helping others always brought him spiritual peace.

One day, he was fixing a loom machine with some other spirits when Thereza appeared. She was jovial again, beautiful, with those sparkling eyes that he had never forgotten while he was there.

"Thereza!"

"Alvaro!"

The two spirits embraced, radiating a sphere of love and goodwill, in a meeting long awaited by both.

"I've never heard from you!" he says, moved.

"From you, I had all the time, since the time you were incarnated. I said many prayers, just as our grandson and other friends, such as those at the Spiritist Center, said prayers for both of us. I am extremely happy for your presence in the Colony."

"And you, where are you?"

"I am in a higher sphere, doing other work. Perhaps you have already been informed that I came on a mission for you. This was really the objective, let's say it was a last chance to change your course as far as moral elevation is concerned."

"And what led you to do this for me?"

"Many lifetimes ago, you saved my life. This moratorium that you yourself gave me, through divine intervention, allowed me to make a very important spiritual change, in that incarnation. Then, as there was an opportunity to help you in this incarnation, I volunteered to return to Earth, to accompany you."

"So you and I were destined?"

"Yes, as to this fact, undeniably. Your fate in wanting to improve materially would bring you to Florianópolis. And my need to acquire new knowledge and somehow contribute to others through charity, were also catalyzing factors."

"Well, I guess I was the lucky one here," said Alvaro, laughing.

"Indeed, you were. But I was the lucky one, hundreds of years ago, and it's a pity, that at least now, you are still not allowed to access other lives or other incarnational planes of the past."

"And where will you go?"

"I am to reincarnate on Earth, when it is in the stage of regeneration. I will stay for a long time in the plane above your colony, where I am, with the most diverse tasks. As for you, I hope you are mature enough to understand that you will no longer incarnate on Earth. My goal was really your change while still on the incarnational plane."

"So your mission failed?"

"Not at all, free will always belongs to the spirit. I went out of dedication; I took care of our children, which is always wonderful. We will not meet for a few tens or even thousands of earthly years, except in the intervals of disincarnation. On more evolved planets, or perhaps the Earth itself, yes. There are bigger debts on your part, to pay up."

"Yes, I know. Everything is up to me to do the best. Let's go forward, always forward. I will always carry you in my heart."

"It's true, you always carry people in your heart until the moment when incarnation occurs. depending on the level of the orb, the veil of oblivion is present. But for all spirits, regardless of who they are, at a certain moment, this veil is no longer imposed on us, but is stripped away."

"And Mom and Dad, have you had any news?"

"Yes, they are fine. Your father, I talked to him once or twice. Your mother, a little more. There are more ancient ties between them and me than you can imagine, even more than with you."

"Can you send them a hug for me?"

"Sure. Maybe you can do that yourself."

"It's true; I should have listened to you Thereza. You were at my side, trying to make me walk the path of the good, and I was totally blind, numbed by money, by success, by influence in business."

"Many are deceived by worldly vices. Do not blame yourself now; the important thing is that it is never too late to start again. Make your new journey a significant source of learning so that you can give your best. With those who will live with you, with the injustices that will be very similar to the ones on Earth, in your future orb. I am eternally grateful to you. Thank you."

"Thank you my dear, you are unique. I love you."

"Me too, and remember, love surpasses frontiers, even spiritual ones."

They hug and say goodbye in an emotional way.

For Alvaro, all the learning may not have been in vain. He made a mistake, fell down, and has the opportunity to get up, even more so with the lessons learned from the error. Maybe the next time he incarnates, he will be more generous, altruistic, more spiritually minded and less carnal.

Seeing Thereza is an important proof that failure brings you to a standstill, but it does not make you go backwards.

Then the memories about the books that Thereza read on Earth come back. Would she have copies of them there? *The Bible, The Spirits' Book, The Gospel according to Spiritism*?

He would ask Hermes, when he saw him.

The earthly years go by and Earth again experiences a deadly disease scenario, this time ravaging the entire globe. The Colony receives hundreds of disincarnated people, disoriented, panting, purplish, short of breath, a reflection of what happened on Earth.

Alvaro is summoned to help receive these spirits, one of the last batches before the period in which the Earth will definitely enter a period of regeneration.

He comforts them, explains to them that life goes on, and that what is happening on Earth is the reflection of human life, materialistic, unbridled, much more in search of pleasure than in the search for moral edification. Moreover, that these events are periodic on planets of trials and expiation.

The buildings and rooms are full. It is necessary to provide new accommodations, better distribution of energetic fluids. There is a greater need for trained spirits to provide emergency assistance to the people who come to this Colony. All the others, in several parts of the world, are at the same work rhythm and positive vibration, in the reception of the disincarnate.

Unfortunately, the Umbral receives a much larger number of disincarnate people at this time. They are even more lost and unassisted because in the planning of a significant portion of them, was the isolation by the virus, blind, dumb and deaf, attacking all the continents in a thousand ways. An invisible war, with thousands of casualties every day.

At the height of the events, both spheres, the upper and lower planes, will receive an unimaginable number of spirits disincarnating at the same time.

In the colonies in particular, there is extensive work of disclosure and preparation for cataclysmic events and Alvaro understands the importance of his work, whatever the activity may be.

He is aware and calm in that he does not deserve the benefits of the regenerated Earth, but the spiritual plane, for him, is a form of training for his future life on earth. Perhaps the selfless love he practices there on behalf of his neighbor will leave some future mark. It is his great faith, which before was very dim or almost non-existent.

In one of the work breaks, he remembers asking Hermes about the books that his wife read on Earth.

"Of course we do. It is from them that we take guidance in our moral edification. The word of God, the teachings of Christ, Kardec's decoding, are enlightening sources of the importance of each spirit, independent of the world. To be a child of God is an unimaginable gift. The higher spirits who have already gone through this transition know very well what that means."

"Where can I get them?" he asks, wanting to read as soon as possible.

"Well, you can borrow them from the library and do your studies. I recommend you read them one at a time, it will help you a lot in your understanding."

"Maybe I've even read some of them in my previous lives."

"Yes, that is true. However, the veil of oblivion, in your case, erases everything. You used to read to instruct yourself, not to truly feed your heart for moral knowledge."

"Thank you, Hermes. Good work for us all!"

"God bless us!"

Unbinding

I, Alvaro, after reading all the books that my wife read and indicated to me, many times in an indirect way, brought myself many certainties.

The first one is that the disincarnation process, or unbinding, is not exactly painful. The body suffers, not the spirit. So much so that more than fourteen earthly years ago I still remember that I had no pain at the moment of disincarnation. I simply fell down and woke up, not exactly in the best place, but in the appropriate place according to my actions.

I was also fortunate that even though I was materialistic, I saw no inheritance fights. There was harmony among my children, which helped me quickly (if that is how we can understand it) regarding my detachment for my accumulation of goods and money.

Different spirits do not have the same fate as mine: they see their burial, others watch their body decompose, and finally, many of them do not even go to the Umbral. I have been able to verify in all these years that there are selfless workers who visit the houses and expel spirits that try to bother more vulnerable incarnates, which is a great truth.

When incarnated, I had the opportunity to hear this in a lecture that my wife watched on TV. Obviously, here in the colony, I could attest to the veracity of such facts.

If planet Earth were more evolved, the people who now reside in this final moment would better understand that death is not an end, but a means. A wonderful school, to put into practice all that we have lived and justly forgotten, through the veil of oblivion. When it is time for a test, you cannot cheat, and the same is true in incarnated life.

I had contact with my parents in the meantime. It was a wonderful meeting, at which I told them all the observations I had learned here. They enjoyed it immensely and thanked me for the opportunity to be their son. I reciprocated in the same way, they were very important, and I asked them that if it were possible, if there was a chance through divine providence, that we would try to walk together.

Mom does not think this is impossible. I also asked about Bruna, since I was not granted the possibility of visiting Earth.

According to them, all our incarnated relatives are well. Thanks to my wife's efforts, everyone understands the efforts she made to spread spirituality to the family nucleus.

Bruna is 71 years old. My children are in middle age. They all talk to each other, even organizing visits and trips together.

As for them, many debts are already settled. Perhaps, I will still be here when they disincarnate and I hope to have the joy of meeting them.

About the Author

Mauro Paes Corrêa is a writer, with publications in other areas of literature, professor and writes since 2006 in several newspapers in southern Brazil, active in various social causes for the benefit of others. Spiritist since the age of fourteen, with personal revelations and student of Allan Kardec's doctrine.

www.ingramcontent.com/pod-product-compliance
Lightning Source LLC
LaVergne TN
LVHW012110160826
845678LV00014B/3024

* 9 7 8 6 5 0 0 3 9 8 5 5 7 *